PET MOTEL

KITTY KING

with

M.A. COBB

ALSO BY KITTY KING

THE COLOR SERIES

Red Night: Special Edition (Book 1)

Red Night: Xavier's Delight

Blue Film (Book 2)

White Hole (Book 3)

Yellow Road (Book 4)

STANDALONE

The Wrong Man

Shared With His Friends

Pet Motel

THE COMPASS SERIES

Beastly Armory (Book 1)

Rawest Venom (Book 2)

Southpaw Slots (Book 3)

Anorthic Anarchy (Book 4)

Full list on author's website:

https://www.kittykingauthor.com/

For information contact: http://kittykingauthor.com

Editing by Indie Editing

Cover design by Kitty King

ASIN: 979-8-9880503-9-1 (eBook)

ISBN: 978-1-964647-09-8 (Paperback)

First Edition: September 2024

10 9 8 7 6 5 4 3 2 1

For those who want to be treated like a caged animal, hold your tongue, and try not to scream.

AUTHOR'S NOTE

Dark erotic horror. Not a romance. She's trapped and treated like a bad dog. And sometimes like a good girl. Feel free to look up content warnings on author's website:

kittykingauthor.com

CHAPTER 1

I am the destroyer. The demolisher of my own destiny. Like a toddler standing near a block tower, I just have to knock myself down.

Insight does nothing when I'm on a Ferris wheel of my own problems. Because if I turn this car around right now, I know exactly where I'll go.

Straight to Brandon's house.

I'll bang on the door, and his wife will open it and yell at me more, her little squirrel face screwed up with hatred. He'll look disgustingly good, but embarrassed, then tell me it's over, to leave them alone. Again. Maybe his babies will be in the background, screaming for their dad.

And I'll do something ridiculous, like meltdown on their porch in a wallowing pile of wreckage. Their wedlock is a reflection of the rubble of my relationship with the love of my life.

Blinking back tears so I can focus on the road, I clear my throat and grab a swig of the water bottle in the center cup holder.

Where I'm heading, I'm not really sure. Just *away*. Because if I turn this car around right now, I *won't* go back to my husband.

"How could you do this to us? You ruined everything. I could kill you right now, you understand that? I don't think I've ever hated you more."

Oh, Zack. I have you beat there.

"Leave. Right now. I can't stand to look at you. We'll talk later."

Stuffing a bag as fast as my hands could grab at things, he followed me around the house, monitoring everything I was taking. *"Yeah, I know. Everything is yours. I get it. I won't take your precious jewelry."* But when he turned his back in disgust, I did. Snagged his grandmother's diamond ring and all the cash in his nightstand drawer, too. That's what he gets for kicking me out of the house.

The house, like I had any money when he married me to pay for it.

JEN

Where r u?

When I don't answer my best friend, she calls. Clenching my jaw, I stare out at the highway and press answer. "Yeah?"

"Oh my god, Cerise. Where are you? What did you do? What happened?"

My chest tightens, and I think about just yanking the wheel hard to the left, barreling into the ditch and dying. Maybe I could just get injured and wake up with amnesia. Start over somewhere new.

"Brandon said it was over."

"Yeah, he says that every week."

A literal sob escapes and the tears follow it. "This time, he meant it. He told his wife everything. He went back to her."

Silence hits the other end of the line as I try to contain myself and keep the car in my lane. Finally, Jen speaks. "I mean… I know you don't want to hear this, but this is probably a very good thing for you. *And* Zack."

Sniffling, I search for some old napkins in the door pocket. "Yeah. I confessed everything to Zack. He kicked me out."

"What? Oh my god, Cerise. Are you coming over?"

Shaking my head, I wipe my nose and tell her. "No. I'm just driving." I don't want to answer her questions. Because I don't know the answers.

"Where?"

"I'll call you later and let you know. Bye, Jen." As soon as I hang up, I push the button to lower my window, grab the phone, and toss it outside. Glancing in my rearview, I see the semi-truck passing me drive over it.

And life feels lighter for the first time since I met Brandon eighteen months ago.

I could be one of those van women. The kind that lives alone without technology. Maybe squat in campgrounds. There's enough cash in my bag to last for at least a year of that, then another two once I hock the ring.

Finally, as if the universe has decided to help me for once, I pass a sign for an upcoming city. They'll probably have a place for me to switch out cars. That will give me even more money.

Pulling onto an exit, I easily find several used car lots down the main strip of whichever small town I've stumbled upon. One has some Ford vans in the back of the lot when I roll past a few fast-food spots. Despite the smell of grilled beef, I'm not hungry.

Instead, I turn into one of the lots and gather all my stuff up, shoving everything into my purse and weekender bag, then step out. Marching straight into the small glass building, I must interrupt the lunch hour as the two older men stop eating their sandwiches to stare at me with wide eyes.

"You need help, ma'am?"

"Yes, please. I want to trade my car in for one of those vans in the back."

Their eyes venture behind me and one drops his lettuce when his jaw unhinges. "That's a Mercedes."

Nodding, I cross my arms. "I know. So, it should be a fine trade-in, then."

After them trying to jerk me around on the prices and so forth and me not caring, wanting to get out of there, I finally get away three hours later with a new ride and a little extra money.

As soon as I push on the gas, some level of comfort soothes my soul for the first time in months. When I get back on the highway, life feels lighter.

I could be anyone.

I can be different this time.

Turning on the radio, I flip it to a country music station. Something Cerise never liked. But maybe *Cherry* does. Perhaps, eventually, I'll enjoy it if I listen long enough.

My optimism lasts for only half an hour before the sky opens up and showers down on me as the light fades into night. At that moment, my stomach cramps from not eating all day. And I feel parched from not having any water. I've never been good at taking care of myself. Probably some leftover parental issue I should discuss with a therapist I'll likely never see.

Not used to steering such a massive vehicle, it swerves in some slick puddles at a high traffic speed. I haven't seen an exit in miles and don't know where I am, other than further west from where I started. The tires on the van won't grip the road the way my car did, and I slow down to try to gain some control. A truck almost rams into the back of me when I do, and I scream, gripping the wheel just as he switches lanes to avoid the collision.

I can't see anything except for my frightened green eyes in the rearview mirror, lit up by passing headlights.

My chest aches from the panic rising within me. The windshield is so caked with water, it looks like a Monet painting. Once the traffic blows past me, there's nothing. I'm alone on a deserted highway in a thunderstorm.

Carefully, I urge the van along while squinting past the squealing wiper blades. Relief floods my soul when a large, green sign appears, indicating an exit. Maybe I can pull over and try to get some rest until the weather passes.

As I crawl off the ramp and make a right, the low fuel light comes on. It would be perfect timing, except the entire area looks deserted. There are no stops, but I keep pushing for a mile or two, spotting a light up ahead. Maybe there is a town nearby with a gas station.

Darkness surrounds me on the little two-lane road, cushioned by trees so large it feels as if they are crushing in on me, especially with the weight of the rain on their leaves. My pulse pounds in my throat, and my vision isn't just blurry from the water spraying across the glass. The tears well up on the rims of my eyes again as fear almost consumes me.

I was stupid to think I could do this on my own. Part of me thinks about just turning around and begging Zack to take me back.

Lost in my thoughts, it must take longer to reach anything because the engine sputters and shuts off when I'm coming around a curve.

"No!" I scream and slam my palms against the steering wheel, but I let off the brake and coast so I can try to pull over somewhere that doesn't look like I'll fall into a ditch. Fortunately, I'm on a downslope, and as I round the corner, a dimly lit neon sign comes into view. It's barely visible between sheets of bad weather pouring over the van, but it's there. And it's a savior.

Pert Motel.

Except the “r” seems to be blown out, and it looks like “Pet Motel”. I don’t have any pets with me, but hopefully I can stay somewhere warm for the night instead of this metal trap.

Glaring intermittently, the red glow of the vacant sign spreads across the droplets like tiny prisms, and I roll across the pavement and into an empty spot. The only car in the entire lot.

Snatching everything I now own, I toss my bags over my shoulders and scurry out of the van. Almost slipping on the pavement, I sprint under the little overhang in front of a glass door that says “Office”.

It’s as old inside as the rooms look from the outside, with faux wood-paneled walls and the smell of ancient cigar smoke clinging to the orange shag carpet. Plastic green chairs line the wall under the front window. Behind the tall counter is a thin wooden door, probably leading to an inner room for the staff.

Shivering, I try to shake off some of the wetness and rub my hands together, wondering if I should call out to see if someone is working tonight or not. Just as I spy a bell, a tall man steps out from the back room, wiping his hands on a paper napkin, which he then uses to dab at his thin goatee.

He’s probably about ten years older than me, maybe in his early forties, and has light brown hair that’s longer in the back. His thin body sways out to the desk, but his cut muscles peek out from his black T-shirt when he reaches for a binder. Behind blue-tinted glasses, his eyes crinkle at the corners as he scans me without inflection, his entire vibe like something that would be in fashion around the time the motel was built.

“You look lost.” A deep voice greets me along with a

broad smile, and the cheeriness of it makes him somewhat attractive, covering up all the other outdated pieces of him.

Giving a polite fake laugh, I ask, "Do you have rooms available?"

"Have ten of them. Ten rooms, ten availabilities." Shrugging slightly, his grin turns a bit shy as he produces a book and opens it to a blank page. "Set those bags down and I'll get one ready for you. Turn on the heater and make sure it doesn't smell too musty in there."

Letting my Louis Vuitton fall off my shoulder, I take a deep breath. He seems quite helpful and respectful, but I keep my purse tucked into my side.

He bends to grab the leather handle, keeping a distance from my body, like he's purposeful in letting me know he's not a threat. Despite that, I take a step away as he stands. When he shoves on the door, he says, "I'll be right back. It's thirty for one night. Five hundred for the month." Pausing, his eyes peek at my ass, tucked away in my cut-off denim shorts, for a moment before he gives me a small wink, then heads outside.

Maybe I'm a fool for doing this. I ran away without a plan and didn't even stop for a burner cell or gas. Hopefully, this man leaves me alone and I can get a good night's rest and decide what my next step should be with some clarity in the morning.

Slipping some cash out of my wallet, I plop the correct amount of bills on top of the book and sign "Cherry Jour" as my name under "guest". Cerise Day doesn't exist right now, but my pulse races at the thought of the attendant asking for my identification. Maybe he won't.

In a few minutes, he returns, keeping his eyes respectfully above my neck.

Spotting the cash, he nods and then reads my name

upside down while writing out a hand printed receipt, but before he finishes, I wave him off.

"Oh, I don't need one." I don't want a paper trail in case Zack sends anyone to look for me. If I'm going to be Cherry, may as well actually do this.

He pauses his writing, then sets the pen down and tilts his head ever so slightly. "On the run, huh?"

A breath catches across my lips at his insinuation. "No! I—"

"Oh, I'm just messing with you." His broad smile returns with a slight chuckle. "If you need anything, I'm Andy, and you can call one on your phone. Check out time, *well,* if we actually had one, is ten." Turning to a cork board behind him, he grabs a key with a large plastic number one on it and lays it on the register. "Your room is all set up for you. Enjoy your evening."

Embarrassingly, as I snag the key, my stomach takes that opportunity to growl so loud, Andy and I meet each other with stunned gazes. My hand clasps my abdomen, but he just gives me an empathetic smile.

"Do you want some snacks?" He tosses his head toward the open door behind him, his long hair waving like he's in a conditioner commercial. "I have a granola bar and water in the back."

Swallowing, I try to peer inside, but it's dark. "Um, okay." Please don't make me go get it. That doesn't seem safe.

Fortunately, he goes into the room on his own and returns with a packaged snack and sealed bottle. Relief floods my body. I hadn't realized how hungry I was until now. "Thanks, Andy."

"No problem, Cherry." The heat behind his eyes as my name forms on his wide lips makes my stomach flip, and not just from how empty it is. There's something about Andy that's mysterious, dangerous, and dark. His sunny demeanor hides something, and I'm not sure I want to stay long enough to find out what.

When I reach the glass door, he says, "Goodnight." I almost jump, but give him a small nod in return.

Once I settle inside the dated room, I rip open the bar and hurriedly eat it, then chug the bottle of water. It's cozy inside with the heater blowing hot air intermittently. Andy set my bag on top of the Formica dresser for me. The television must be original, but I'm not planning on watching anything. All I want is a hot shower, then bed.

The bathroom is unexpectedly clean. Sure, everything's old, but it's functional. Pulling my white blouse over my head, I get a peek in the mirror and realize… it's been perfectly see-through. My red, lacy bra shows everything, and embarrassment flushes my olive cheeks, thinking about Andy seeing it all. Fortunately, my freckles cover my chagrin somewhat. When I unplait my shoulder length, brown hair, it's soaking wet. Hopefully, there's some shampoo in the shower.

Fortunately, there is, and the water gets hot enough for me to feel scrubbed and fresh after a long day. Slipping into a pair of sleep shorts and a tank top, I slide under the starched sheets, my curly hair still a bit damp. No matter. I'm too exhausted and heartbroken to care what I look like.

The humming sound of the window unit lulls me into a quick sleep, but I have a nightmare about a tall man looming over me while I slumber. Something in my subconscious tells me to wake up, that I'm in danger.

My eyes snap open to a shadowy figure lying over me, and as I scream, he slaps a hand across my mouth. Gripping my arm and pulling it out, he shoves a needle into it as I thrash against his solid body.

Like struggling through deep water, I can't move, and it gets even more difficult as the world fades to black.

I am the slayer of my own sanity.

CHAPTER 2

Pain is all I know.

Well, I guess when I imagine "pain", I think of sharp sensations of agony. This is more of a dull ache that I get some relief from for a moment, only to be reminded of it again when I move.

Uncomfortable.

That's more appropriate. Like my body doesn't really *fit* anywhere. But if I contort it like it's supposed to be, I'm not sure that would feel any better.

Groaning, I open my eyes, memories of the last day flooding back to my mind. Sheer horror beseeches my eyes when I take in my surroundings and the reason I'm so sore.

Releasing a guttural scream, it comes out as a coarse, pathetic attempt for help.

I'm stuck in a wire crate, like one we had for Gigi, our Golden Retriever, when I was growing up. Underneath me is a plastic floor covered with a dirty newspaper. I must have wet myself at some point because it's soaked with dark yellow urine.

But what's most disconcerting is my outfit. Or lack

thereof. Around my waist is something that looks like a skirt but showcases my nakedness completely underneath and has a long tail attached to the waistband. My nipples are only warmed by small pasties, but my hands and feet have padded leather mittens and socks on them.

When I lift my hands to my tender neck, I tug on a hard collar that's tightened so much it's almost difficult to swallow.

I can barely sit, but lean at an angle to grasp at the bars surrounding me, attempting to pry them apart. They're too strong for me in my weakened state, and my head pounds harder from lack of food, water, and whatever drug Andy injected me with.

The room looks like a basement constructed of plain concrete cinder blocks. Light comes from humming fluorescent lights overhead and one small window high up on the wall across from me. To my left is a wooden staircase leading up somewhere behind a wall and next to the window is a solid wood door that probably leads outside.

Hazy glass fogs the view, but the sky seems gray and overcast. It must be either the morning after I arrived or late evening, and it's still raining.

My heart thuds hard in my chest when I spy more crates like mine lined against a side wall. Dark stains linger underneath them, and a floor drain sits in the middle of the room.

A shadow crawls down the steps with heavy footfalls lumbering as a figure emerges from above. Andy's smiling face greets me like I'm checking in at the front desk.

"What did you do?" I can barely speak, my throat is so dry. How long has it been since I had water? Food? As if in reply, my stomach growls, twisting in on itself with hunger. "Let me out!" Grasping at the bars, I shake the crate as much as I can, trying to loosen the door, the wires, something. My mitts prevent me from gaining a decent grasp.

"Aw, puppy. Look at you trying to speak like a human. That's so cute." From behind his back, he produces a rolled-up newspaper and smacks my knuckles. Fortunately, it doesn't hurt much, the leather protecting me, but it's enough to make me sit back and gasp at his absolute insanity. "Oh, you soiled your paper. Well, we'll take you outside and let you tinkle so you learn to go potty on the grass."

"What? Are you crazy?"

Andy's face clouds with darkness, and he swiftly grasps the top of my crate, rattling it violently. Scurrying to the back of it, I try to get as far away from him as I can. His eyes, almost black behind his glasses, narrow as he calmly speaks in his resonating tenor. "Now, you'll behave, or I'll let you die in there without food or water. Do you understand?"

Terror floods my soul for the first time. I have no doubt he means exactly what he says. Those empty crates are maybe a testament to it. Sitting back on my thighs, I stare at him. Despite something charming about his face and the hypnotic nature of his voice, he's petrifying.

Andy lowers his glasses down the bridge of his nose and gives me a wide smile, showcasing a perfect set of white teeth and two dimples above his goatee. "Good girl. If you're obedient enough, I'll give you a name. Now… let's go outside to potty, then you can have your breakfast."

Relaxing back so he can let me out of this tiny crate, I loosen my muscles in preparation for a fight as soon as he opens the door. He squats near the end and pulls a leash out from his pocket. Like I'm a fucking dog. I guess that's what the tail is for.

As soon as he slides the lock, I lunge forward, but he grabs my neck with one hand and slings me onto the ground until I land on my back. He holds me down by stepping on my stomach as I let out a cry. His boot bears into me until I still under his weight, hoping he doesn't crush me. "Don't move or you'll get really hurt. Do you understand?"

Glancing at his eyes, I hold in position, and his grin returns. "Good girl. Ugh, I can tell you're gonna love your master soon." Bending forward, he clips the leash to my collar. It slips through the mittens when I try to grab it. With a firm yank, he tugs me forward until I'm on my knees. When I attempt to rise, he stops me. "On all fours like a good puppy."

I must be slow about it because he uses the end of the chain leash to smack my stomach until I bend forward onto my hands.

"Let's go, puppy."

I crawl toward the door where he leads us. When the door opens, cold hits my skin like knives as the rain drops drizzle, causing me to shiver. Heaving in a small breath, my knees take the brunt of all the pebbles on a small set of stone steps. It leads us out from an old cedar house on a steep hill overlooking the motel. Relief makes my shoulders relax as I hit the grass and soft mud at the top. Guiding me to the middle of a small yard with a cliff edge, he points to the ground. "Go potty."

My "paws" won't grip the slippery ground, but I try to take in as much of my surroundings as I can to escape later. Trees line the sides and back of the house, while a long gravel drive leads down the hillside to the back of the motel. There's absolutely nothing else. I can't make out neighbors or other establishments, even from this height.

I'm definitely alone here.

Fear makes my teeth chatter. This may be my only opportunity to relieve myself, so I spread my legs and do. Fortunately, Andy looks away, but part of me wishes he didn't. Like he needs to see how disgusting this is. Maybe if it bothers him enough, he'll leave me alone and not do what it is I think he may do to me later. But I have a feeling this is not going to end as well as I hope.

"I-I need toilet paper. This isn't hygienic," I tell him. Will it matter to him if I stink before he tries to rape me? I guess there are worse things.

Hopefully this isn't part of some body part factory. Kidney donation service. Maybe I'll just be his pet plaything until I can get out of here.

"You can earn that, but for now, I'll clean you up. Let's go." With a snap on the leash, he tugs me toward the house. As we approach the stairs, he pauses and grabs a water hose lying next to the door. When he does, I lift my paws in front of my face just as he turns the spray on my back side. The water is freezing, and a silent scream wrenches from my chest at the pressure and shocking temperature.

Trembling, I think I'll do anything for toilet paper. Or, better, an indoor toilet. No, better, Cerise would be in her warm home away from this crazy man and horrific place. Even with everything I left behind, I regret all my life's decisions that lead me here.

"Move, let's go."

On shaky knees, I stumble and follow him into the basement. The back wall I couldn't see before is covered in various BDSM equipment, including hooks and chains. A small alcove juts off of it and holds one wooden door. I wonder what's behind it. Please don't be a slaughter room.

Nearing the crate, Andy shoves me in with his hands all over my ass. I scurry inside as quickly as I can and sit. "Such a good girl. You hungry? You a hungry hamster?"

I'm starving and so thirsty by now, I feel physically ill. My throat is raw and my body weak. My head still reels from the drugs. If I could have water, I think I'd feel so much better. Maybe even have the strength to fight him off or escape.

Grabbing some bars of my crate, he pulls them apart

slightly, then rubs the front of his jeans for a moment. My eyes follow his movements carefully as he undoes his belt, then unzips. My stomach knots up, and not from hunger. Oh no. Where is this going?

Without even a change in his half-smiled expression, he pulls out a veiny, hard cock, then runs it along the bars on the top. I watch it like it's a snake about to bite. "You're a hungry hamster, aren't you?"

If I bite it off, maybe I can get away… No, that's dumb. He'd get pissed off and keep me in here longer. Right?

"You want to eat? You gotta feed off this first. Show me how hungry you are. Suck me off, pet."

Despite being almost delirious with hunger, I consider just dying here to avoid taking him inside my mouth. Gathering up some courage, I stick out my tongue. Andy releases a breathy chuckle while rubbing his cock across the bars, the sound like a xylophone. His looming presence makes me twitch from some combination of fear and the ice settling over my prickled skin. My mouth is so dry, this can't be very pleasant for him, and some satisfaction secretly hides in my heart thinking about that.

"Open wider," he says, and the corners of my lips crack as I do. Pursing his lips, he spits inside my mouth.

I slam it closed and yell. "Ew!" Disgusting!

"Puppy, you want your breakfast? Open up for me. Feed off me. Show me what a hungry hamster you are. You need your master to live."

Frustrated, angry, and filled with heat, I sit on my heels and open wide for him. He shoves his granite length between the bars, and I attach myself to it while meeting his eyes. I must look like a gerbil at a bottle feeder with how much I suckle on his dick.

"Yes, puppy. Good girl, just like that. Focus those beautiful green eyes on my face, pet. Such a *gorgeous* puppy."

Thrusting his hips in and out, he hits the back of my throat until I gag. If I had any way to make tears, I would cry. "Curl your tongue around me, pup. Stroke me and get your meal."

Pinching a few wires, he squeezes his long fingers inside the crate and grabs my collar, pulling me closer to his waist. My nose smushes against his abs until I can't breathe. His musk is so potent I lurch and try to slink back, but he's got me in a tight grip. Lifting my paws, I press against my cage. It doesn't help. With the rise in my pulse and flutter inside my chest, I scream around his girth. Finally, I close my jaw tightly around his muscle.

"Oh, you want to play *that* game?" Releasing my collar, I fall back, and he snaps open the cage door with a resounding click. He grabs a handful of my hair and drags me out onto the concrete floor. Screaming and kicking, I twist in his grasp, but he's got such a tight hold on me, every resistant movement of mine hurts worse.

Kneeling, I scramble with him to avoid getting my hair ripped out of my scalp as he presses me into the wall of toys. He snatches a pair of pliers from the tool holder and tugs my collar until I sit in front of him. Using every ounce of muscle I have, I lean away from him as much as I can.

"Please, please don't hurt me. I'm sorry, please," I beg.

Around the base of his cock is a fresh red mark, something I now deeply regret giving him. Gripping my collar with one hand, he pinches my nose while holding the pliers in the other. Pressure builds until I know I have to open my mouth to breathe. When I do, he clutches my cheeks so hard, I can't shut my jaw, then he digs into my mouth with the rusty pliers and finds a back tooth and begins pulling.

Trying to scramble back from him, I meet the concrete, the pain and pressure too much. Moaning and screaming around his hands, I push against his immovable thighs. Sobs and dry wails rumble from my chest, but he keeps up his mission until the tooth cracks, then breaks into my mouth, the shards almost going straight down my throat. Blood spurts onto my arid tongue. It's a welcome relief from the pain of him trying to tear the tooth from my head.

His nails scrape against my throat as he wrenches me by the collar and tosses me back into the crate once again, then slams the door. He tosses the pliers aside and says, "Lose another if you do that again. I asked you nicely if you wanted breakfast, but I guess you don't. Starve in there for all I care."

Turning on a heel, he walks casually to the staircase.

"Andy, please," comes out hoarse and mumbled from my aching mouth. "Please give me water."

He pauses, then continues upstairs. A door slams shut, and then the lights are turned off.

I'm going to die here.

CHAPTER 3

How am I still alive? Is it my thoughts that keep me so?

No. My heart still thuds in my chest, *hard* against the ribs like it wants to escape. Hunger left me hours ago, but thirst is making me see strange things in the darkness.

At one point, I dreamt of the beach with Zack. We honeymooned in Greece, and I remember the feeling of being *intoxicated* on his love. When I really think about it, I never stopped loving him. It's just when Brandon came along and gave me more attention, things felt *fresh* and new again. I'd captured that honeymoon feeling and bottled it up, and it was there for me whenever Brandon fucked me.

Except it was all a mirage. And I fell for it.

It's probably better for Zack that I'm here, close to death. I'm not sure I deserved him. Even if I did, I don't now. Not after what I put him through.

A scraping sound hits my ears, but I'm too weak to sit up, even when the light blares into my eyes, causing them to snap shut.

"Pet? Love? Are you still alive?" It's Andy. Not sure who

else I expected. Maybe the police? Would Zack have sent anyone to find me?

It's impossible to swallow. I think my mouth stopped making spit ages ago.

"Oh! Look at you! *Well*… you pretty thing. You're a fighter." He kneels at the crate door and slides the lock open. "Won't do no good pleasuring me if you can't sit up, though. Let's get you some water so you can get some breakfast."

Shoving a dog dish into the crate with me, he smiles like he's my hero while I lift my head enough to watch him pour a bottle of water in it.

Who knew water had such an appetizing *smell*? Not even hesitating, I open my mouth as he splashes it in, then stick my face to the bottom of the metal bowl and slurp. As much as my tongue can hold, I toss it to my throat, relief hitting my senses. With each swallow, my brain functions faster. Thoughts seem clearer.

"Now. You gonna be a good girl or we gotta remove more of them teeth?" My tongue hits the jagged pieces left in my gums.

Barely able to speak, my hoarse voice shreds the stale air. "I'll be good." I need to eat, gather up some strength, then get the fuck out of here somehow.

"I like that. I knew you were smart. Crawl to me, pet. Come on out here. You've earned some exercise."

Pulling myself up by the wires of the crate, I sluggishly force my knees to move forward as my paw gloves slap the ground. Everything hurts. And I don't care anymore. I just want food.

Hooking a finger in my collar, he tugs me close to his crotch, then unzips. "Get me hard and then drink my cum, pet."

Licking his dick all over, I plunge myself onto him, hoping it doesn't take long to get him off. "Ugh, such a good girl. What a good little girl you are." Stroking under my chin, he uses his hand to lift my face, so I have to stare into his eyes while servicing him. "That's it. Worship me. Show me what a good pet you are. Who's your master?"

Moaning around him, I don't really say anything, but force myself harder as he grows within my mouth.

"I didn't hear you. Who is your master?" Gripping the crown of my head by the hair, he tugs me off his length. Drool drips from my mouth. All that wasted water…

"You," I pant out.

His eyes brighten behind his dark glasses and a large smile forms across his broad lips. "You *are* a good girl. Yes, my little girl. I think I could fall in love with you." My stomach lurches at that thought as he thrusts into my mouth once more. Of course, if I got him to have feelings for me, maybe I could get away sooner.

Straightening my posture, I give him some sultry eyes. His cock throbs against my tongue as I taste a salty drop of pre-come. "Fuck… you're so beautiful. Take this big dick and swallow, pet. Show me how hungry this little hamster belly is."

Ropes of bitter cum spurt down my throat, and I almost gag, having not eaten anything for days. But I pull back enough to snap my lips closed and swallow while trying to give him a sexy expression. He seems a bit dazed from his post-orgasm high. Gathering himself, he zips up his jeans.

Using the back of my leather mitt, I wipe my chin. "Can-can I have some food now, Andy?"

"Yes, pet. Let me look at you for a moment." Tilting his head, his light brown hair flows over his shoulder, and he strokes a crooked finger against my cheek. *Lovingly*. Like I'm a prized possession. It makes me feel odd. Like a mixture of abhorrence and arousal. My nipples peak to buds covered only by the pasties. I'm glad he can't see.

"Crawl into your crate, and I'll get your breakfast." My eyes dart to the backdoor as he moves to the hallway. Could I run? There's no way. He'd be on me faster than I could escape. I can barely scoot.

Doing just as he says, I return to my new home as he presents me with another dish. This one is filled with actual dog food nuggets. Or what smells like it.

"Let me get you fresh water." When he places the kibble next to the other dish, he pats my head. This fucker is insane.

"Y-you want me to eat dog food?"

"Puppies can't eat people food… unless they are good girls. Good girls that obey their masters can have food off the counter and sleep in a real bed." Closing the crate, he stands over me as if waiting to watch me eat.

I have no shame anymore. Starving, delirious, I dip my face in and grab a chunk and chew.

"If you mix some water in, it'll soften it. But… do you want to be a good girl for me?"

"What does that mean?"

Crossing his arms, he smirks. "That means obeying your master. Doing just what you're told. Learning new tricks. And, when your time is right, growing a litter of pups in that belly."

My jaw drops and a kernel of food rolls out onto the floor. "Wh-what?" If he's going to try to impregnate me, I'll just have to tell him it's not possible. He doesn't need to know it's because of a birth control implant.

"Yes, pet. Don't you want some puppies in that belly?"

"I can't get pregnant."

He freezes, holding his breath, and finally narrows his eyes at me while I hope he buys the lie. "Well… I was really hoping *you'd* work out." With a deep sigh, he frowns. "But I guess then there's no use for you."

My eyes widen as he goes to the wall and grabs a machete

and turns to me. Scrambling back as far as I can, a shrill shriek leaves my lungs. I cry, "No, no! I mean I-I *can* have children, I just… I'm on birth control! That's all I meant." Sobbing, I wail, "Please, *please*. Andy, please don't hurt me."

His steps pause, an unsettling smile crawling over his lips. "That's amazing, pet! *Aww*, Cherry girl, don't cry! I was going to miss you! But you'll stay with me! We'll just have to get rid of your birth control, then, won't we?"

Rubbing my face from the snot dripping down my nose, I watch carefully as he returns his blade to the hook. Nodding, I agree with him, "Yes. Yep. I was taking oral pills and now that I haven't had them, I should become fertile again f-for your puppies." I lie while staring at the plastic floor in my cage.

"Hmm, that's great news. You are being so good today. Do you want to go outside?"

"Yes, please."

Crouching in front of me, he arches an eyebrow. "Sit up and beg like a good pet and say yes again. Say yes to your master."

Squatting as much as I can, I raise my paws up like a dog. "Yes, master."

"Good girl. Let's go."

Fortunately, it's no longer raining as he leads me into the calm afternoon sun by my chain leash. Once we near the lone tree, I do my business and scan the motel parking lot. Still no one. There're no cars passing by, either. This place truly is deserted. No wonder it hasn't changed much since it was built.

"An old state route used to run through here. Some miners lived up in the hollers there, but that's abandoned, too. No, it's miles to the highway. I still got some good buddies I see at the bar in town, though." His eyes scan where mine were spying. In the light, he doesn't look as frightening, almost candidly carefree. Dare I say, attractive for a monster. Catching me looking at him, his lips spread wide, and he says, "But that's a long way aways, too. Nope. It's just you and me, pet." Bending down, he touches my nose with the tip of his finger. "Let's get my Cherry girl a bath. I think you deserve that."

My aching muscles could weep with relief. "O-okay."

Andy guides us around the front of the house and up a wooden painted porch. Next to the right side on the gravel drive is an old Jeep. The front door is glass, and we enter a small foyer with an old living room to our right. His place looks like a grandmother decorated it; the amount of crochet Afghans and yellowed doilies is staggering. Passing an open door, a cozy bedroom with a king-sized bed awaits and a big, plush dog bed sits on the floor next to it.

"That's where you could sleep if you behave," he says with a nod of his head in that direction.

"Yes, master." Scanning the kitchen we pass, I spot a back-door leading out to the driveway and a key rack with a set of keys hanging from it. My heart races as I quickly divert my eyes like I hadn't been forming a plan of escape. Just keep crawling.

We reach a little bathroom, which holds a large porcelain tub. The good kind, made in the mid-century. Once I'm on the tile floor, Andy shuts and locks the door behind me, then ties my leash to a robe hook on the back. He gets the water ready and turns to me with a hand planted on his chin. "Stand up and undress, Cherry girl."

He's already seen everything, so I'm not sure why I'm so nervous. Some of the pain from the last few days is relieved when I stand on shaky knees. Almost losing my balance, I grip the sink as he hurries to put his arms around my waist. Our faces are so close, he could kiss me. A momentary pause passes between us, and I think he may. My breath hitches as my stomach rolls. His breath smells like coffee and chocolate, and part of me thinks it wouldn't be the absolute worst thing to brush my lips against his if I can get a taste of something that isn't kibble.

"Here, let me help you, pet." Loosening my collar, he unlocks my hands, then my feet, and unstraps the pads on them. Once he removes my tail belt, I stand completely naked after he pops off my pasties. "Good girl. Let's get you in the water. Don't shake on me, though." His laugh seems so genuine. Like I'm a child or a real dog.

Placing his warm hand on my back, he guides me over to the water and I step in. Immediately, tears fall from my eyes at the comfort it provides me. It's the first time I've felt like things may be okay in a long time.

Once I settle in, I rest my neck against the back wall and slump down. Without a word, Andy lifts my left arm and uses a loofah to scrub the skin with soap. Then he works on my right arm. Each leg. Between my legs. Every circular motion feels better than the expensive masseuse I pay for every month.

"Sit for me."

Cracking an eye open, I see him with a bottle of shampoo in his hand. I swivel and curl my knees to my chest as he works my hair into a lather. It smells like citrus and pine, and I think if I got close enough to him, that would be his scent. As he works my head, shoulders, neck, back… I doze off.

It's been days since I've fallen asleep, and the slumber is so deep, it may take years to wake me.

When I do, I'm pinned to a hard surface, lying on my back. My bent arms are held in chains above my head, and my legs are spread wide, held in similar restraints. The fluorescent lights of the basement glare above me. Almost choking around a gag tied inside my mouth, I attempt to lift my neck to see where Andy is. His smiling face peeks into my view.

"You lied to me, pet."

My brow furrows as I shake my head slowly.

Holding up a scalpel, it shines as he lets it dance between his fingers. "You have a birth control implant in your arm."

Screaming through the rubber ball, I try to tell him to stop what he's about to do.

"You may want to go back to sleep for this," he says…

Then he plunges it into my arm.

CHAPTER 4

I think I passed out from the pain. And when I'm aware again, I get flashes of Andy digging into my arm with a scalpel and hear myself crying, then faint again. Blood, sharp anguish, and terror I've never experienced hit me until I'd rather die.

Why was I fighting so hard to stay alive? What a fool I was.

When I finally wake, he's pouring water over my arm. My eyes peek to see the wound stitched up shoddily with some black thread. Whimpering, I try to squirm from the ache, but can't move.

Andy reaches over and lifts my eyelids with his thumbs as I scream at his sudden movement. Trying my hardest, I can't blink against his force.

"Now. Let's get something straight. I don't like liars. I felt your little birth control implant in there. And you could have woken up missing an arm. But I don't want no three-legged dog." Hocking up phlegm from the back of his throat, he spits it into my screaming mouth, and I quickly shut it and sob. "Do you understand?"

Nodding as much as I can, he finally lets me go, my eyes burning from staying open for so long. Clamping them shut, I listen to his footsteps move away, then return. A sharp burning pain hits my pussy until I lurch forward with a cry.

"You want to lie? Then you're gonna get spanked." Another swat makes my stomach squeeze at the sensation. "Yes, focus on your pain. Turn that brain off and think of me." Andy walks around my body and strokes black leather strips of a flogger through his hand.

No matter how hard they want to close, my knees are locked in place, and when he marks me another time, I just lie back and take it with a wailing cry. And again. And one on my stomach until my screams lash out as sharp as the leather.

"Please, Andy."

He smacks the weapon into his palm, preparing for another hit. "Please, what, pet?"

"I-I'll do anything." At this point, I will. Escape, food, water, comfort, nothing else matters except that the pain stops. If he wants me to suck his cock or get pregnant or swallow his spit, I'll happily do it all.

Andy's still so long, I lower my chin to find him standing between my legs, staring at my body, then my face. His Adam's apple bobs as he swallows. "You'll obey me?"

Drawing in a long stream of air, some of the throbbing between my legs slows to a manageable ache. "Yes."

"Say it, though. Say you'll obey me."

"I-I'll obey you." Lowering his forehead toward me, he gives me a pointed look until I finish with, "Master."

His entire body relaxes as he removes his glasses and tucks them into the top of his T-shirt. Gray eyes crinkle at the corners as he smiles at me. Without the dark shade over his eyes, he seems younger. Almost handsome, which is absolutely terrifying. "I like that. I knew I'd like you, Cherry girl."

I flinch as he grasps an ankle and undoes my bindings,

then the other. When he unlocks my arms, I quickly fold them in and curl into a fetal position on my side. The bench is rugged, but I don't care. The position is a momentary luxury I need before I beg him to cut me up with the machete.

When he hovers next to me, he observes for a long time until I raise my head and ask him, "What do you want me to do?"

"I want you to fuck me like you mean it."

Bewildered, I blink several times. "Huh?"

A small smile forms on his lips, and his eyes grow heavy as they scan my legs. "I want you to convince me how much you want your master. No acting. No *lying*. I want you to give yourself to me." Crossing his arms as if everything he says is perfectly reasonable, he resumes a stoic position.

I had expected rape. Probably painful and brutal. I thought possibly anal without lube. Maybe even have my insides jarred. But fucking him *like I mean it*? This seems impossible. Especially after what he just put me through.

With a smirk, he says, "I mean... if I *don't* believe it, I can always take that arm off for you. Fuck your stump after."

"No!" I yell. "I'll do it. I-I'll fuck you."

"*Make love* to me."

As if he had just slapped me with words, I stare at him with my jaw unhinged. Closing it, I swallow and manage to whisper, "I'll make love to you, Andy."

"Hot diggity dog!" He walks to the end of the bench and grabs his jeans to unbutton them.

Sitting up, I practically spit on him. "But... it would be so much better in a bed." His light gray eyes snap to my face with a question lingering in his expression. "That's how I like to, um, *make love*. In a bed. With the lights off."

Pausing in his motion to release himself, a furrow forms between his brows. "Lights on."

Nodding slowly, I keep my gaze on his. "Okay, master. Lights on."

His palm turns over, and he presents it to me. Does he want me to walk? Hold his hand? As if in answer to my unspoken question, he grabs mine and pulls me off the table. I stumble, but he snags my naked waist with his bare arm. "Whoa, girl. You'll learn to walk on two feet."

Horrifyingly, he then presses his lips to the top of my head.

I was never good at hiding my expressions. And I'm plagued with resting bitch face. But I try to push all of that aside and smile the most genuine one I've ever had.

A vision of Brandon and me at the horse racing track comes to mind. We'd played hooky from work and sneaked away for a fun date day together, one of the few ways we could meet without our spouses knowing. He'd fucked me in the bathroom hurriedly. It was always fast, hard, and passionate.

But my grin falters. The dull ache in my arm moves into my chest.

He's not who I want.

He wasn't there when I had a miscarriage and thought about just dying on my bathroom floor. He didn't bring me cake in bed where I stayed the week after my mom died. I'm not even sure he knows my favorite color.

Zack does.

And so with the thought that I could get back to him, I remember the stony white beaches on our honeymoon and glamor Andy with a beaming expression as we alight the stairs together, hand in hand.

Guiding me into the stuffed bedroom, lit by a dim lamp, he bumps against my bare back, his erection poking me with urgency. I can do this.

When we reach the bed, he spins me by the waist to face

him. His eyes narrow to my mouth. He's waiting, I know. So I give it to him.

Snaking my hands around his neck, I soften my face and press my lips to his. It's strange, the way he tastes. Not like anyone else. Maybe like juniper berries and something metallic. Either way, it's bitter, with a hint of something intoxicating.

His body envelops me, pressing his chest into mine, and I shiver. Possibly because I've been naked so long. I don't remember what it's like to be warm, but also because of the desire he seems to surround me with as he leans into me.

Like I'm someone else.

Maybe he's missing someone just as I am. I can be her. I can show him. If I were with Zack right now, I think I would. Just to prove how much I love him.

So, closing my eyes, I let the heat from Andy's body make me feel comforted, and a tear escapes down my cheek.

He lays me back on the mattress and spreads my knees, never breaking his stare. Leaning up on my elbows, I *think* about what is in his jeans pockets as he undoes them. But if I consider how to escape right now, my concentration will wane.

And I really want to keep my arm, despite how much pain it's in.

He sets his glasses on a nightstand, then rips off his shirt. Lowering his white briefs, his firm dick flops out, pointing right where it wants to go. Taking a deep inhale, I breathe it all out and plaster a smile on my face.

"Please give it to me," I whisper, trying to keep the fear out of my vocal cords.

Standing in front of me, he strokes himself and tilts his head. "How bad do you want me?"

It's a test. I know it is. Steeling my nerves, I wrap my arms around his back, and pull him onto me until his body lingers over mine. "I need you, Andy."

Somehow, I have to make myself wet through this, so I grind on his length using it to hit my clit repeatedly. He lowers his head to watch me move, then thrusts his hips, matching my rhythm, and gives me the friction I need. Dropping his head to my neck, he scrapes the skin with his teeth before sucking, and tingles erupt down my spine. One hand clutching his back and the other his head, I press him into me, partially so I don't have to see his face while I do this.

His breathy pants make me loosen up for him, though, and on one stroke, he meets my entrance with the tip of his cock. Lifting to his elbows, he grasps my face with both of his hands and forces my eyelids to stay open. "Watch me. Don't look away." Reeling back some, he then plunges inside me as his face slackens with ecstasy.

I hate that mine does the same.

Tossing my head back, I let him work inside me, heat reeling in my belly. A bead of sweat drops from his forehead onto my cheek and rolls down. "Look at me while I make love to you," he pants.

Somehow, I've got to convince him of an amazing orgasm. Of course, I've faked them before, but this needs to be the performance of a lifetime. Wrapping myself around him, I use my feet to push him deeper, like I used to do with Zack when we were still having sex.

I miss him.

Gathering Andy's face with my hands, I plunge my tongue inside his mouth. "Mmm, Cherry girl. You taste so good." Something about his voice and the way he looks at me with esteem makes me feel hot inside. "I want to make you come. Please you, so you don't want anyone else. I'll be in charge of your pleasure and pain."

Nodding, I flex my inner muscles around him, pretending I'm there.

But something strange happens. The way his abs hit my clit and the length of him hitting all the right spots makes me think I may not have to fake it. As I feel myself escalating toward that euphoria, I squeeze my face tightly, but he says, "Not yet. You need my permission, pet. Ask me if you can come."

Clenching my teeth, I ask, "Can I come, master?"

His cock gives a throb within my walls. "Only if you tell me you love me."

A sharp breath cuts across my lips as I gasp. "Wh-what?"

"Tell me you love me while you come, Cherry. I need to hear it. Say it."

My stomach tightens in a knot, and I think I may come without him allowing it, but the fear of losing an arm to a machete makes me focus enough that I say, "I love you."

"You love who?"

"I love you, A-andy?"

A smile broadens his face as his pace escalates. Groaning at my words, he instructs, "Say it again. Mean it."

"I love you, Andy."

"Yes, pet. Come and scream how much you love me."

His cock fills me and pulses deep inside as I clench him with my pussy and let out a feral scream, "I love you, Andy!"

The warmth of his cum spills inside as he presses his lips to mine and whispers, "Such a good girl. Good girl for loving your master." Gathering me close to his body, his perspiration coats my skin, and I'm hot all over. He doesn't leave me, though, and uses his softening cock to plug me up, scooting us further onto his bed.

As soon as the waves of my pleasure dissipate…

I want to do it all over again.

CHAPTER 5

The dog bed is more comfortable than the crate, and I'm grateful for it. Despite what I have to do to keep it. He's also allowed me to wear my own panties, because I got my period, as well as one of his T-shirts. I still have to wear the tail and collar. But I get to use his bathroom if I cook his meals and clean for him.

While standing at the stove making his morning eggs, I eye the set of car keys hanging off the wall hooks for the third day in a row. What has it been? A week almost since I've been trapped here? Fear makes me hesitate in grabbing them and sprinting to his Jeep. No, I need a strategic plan. And I have one.

Andy's gone for long periods, and when he goes, he always locks me in my crate. The only time I'm not under his watch is the bathroom. When I bathe, he now allows me some privacy. I sneaked a sweatshirt out of his closet, along with a pair of slippers that almost fit me, and put them behind some coats. Early one morning while he's still asleep, I'll slide into those clothes, use the small silver key to open the back door, and the Jeep key to leave. As soon as I jump in the vehicle, I'll lock the doors and hurry away. I'll leave everything I brought and head to the nearest public place I find.

A sharp snap on my ass startles me from the vision of escape. Andy's face rests on my shoulder as I scramble his meal. "Mm, morning, pet. Smells good." Brushing a finger down my arm, he smiles at me, and I muster as fake of one as I can and give it to him in return. In love, that's what I am… if I want to keep all my parts.

"Morning, master."

"You forgot one thing, didn't you?"

Clearing my throat, I swallow. "Um, you were sleeping, and I—"

"It's okay. Tell me." One of his hands rests against my hip as he moves to stand behind me. A shiver runs down my spine.

"I love you, Andy."

"Good girl. And what did you forget?"

My nipples harden as he hooks a finger in my panties and pushes the crotch aside, along with my pad. "To drain your balls."

Thrusting his hardness between my pussy lips, he releases a heavy sigh on my neck. "That's right, pet. Such a good girl. A loving puppy for me. Hike that leg up."

Turning off the burner, I slide the pan to a cool one and lift my thigh. He doesn't hesitate to fit himself inside my entrance. The confusing part is always how turned on I get when he fucks me. Arching my back, my ass hits his abs as he groans.

"That's it, Cherry girl. You're my little bitch, aren't you? Gonna have my litter?"

Snaking an arm around his neck, I bounce off his length. At least if I'm going to be trapped, treated like a pet and forced to cook and clean, I can take some pleasure from him. "Yes, master."

"Say you want my puppies, bitch."

Grabbing my collar, he tugs back so I can barely breathe. One of his hands swats my outer thigh as I gasp. "I want your puppies."

"You have to come with me, then, pet. And I'll *know* if you fake it. Get off on your master and suck up my cum in that tiny twat of yours." He reaches around and sticks two fingers on my clit. I *hate* that he now knows exactly how to make me melt, and the heat that floods through my abs makes any menstrual cramps I had disappear. Especially when I reach that precipice of pleasure. It rips through me like a habit now. And when I come, I scream, "I love you, Andy."

Gripping my waist, he buries his face into my neck and sniffs. "Oh, fuck. You are such a good girl. Here you go, pet." Growling, he bites my skin until I whimper, the harshness of the sting lessened by my post-orgasm high.

As soon as he unloads within me, he slips out and twirls me to face him. "Mm, clean me up, pet, and then feed me my breakfast."

Glancing at his softening cock, it holds a ring of my blood around it, as well as some mucus strands. When I attempt to grab a paper towel, he laughs and snatches my wrist. "No. With your mouth. On your knees."

My stomach lurches at the thought, but I know I don't have a choice. Slowly lowering myself, I squeeze my eyes closed and feel for his still warm dick. Taking a big breath in, I open wide, but he tilts my chin up before I can hurry and get it over with. "Look at me while you service me. Show me how much you love me."

Looking behind his dark glasses, I hold his gaze and swallow his dick. *It's just blood, Cerise. Calm down. It's sterile.* It tastes of old iron and his bitter semen, as well as my own musk. Just as I think I'll vomit, he slides out of my mouth and helps me stand. His finger hooks underneath the front of my collar as he draws my face close to his.

Slowly, he leans forward and captures my lips with his, his tongue edging inside my mouth. His kiss is warm, soft, but formidable. Especially when he wraps his arms around me like I'm his long-lost love. I even find myself getting lost in it, a dizzy feeling invading my head.

He spanks me to break us apart and gives a chuckle. "Mm, I love mealtime with you. You are the best bitch I ever had." Bouncing on his toes, he tucks himself back in his jeans and zips up.

When we move to the dining table, I take my position between his legs as he sits. My head rests inside of one of his open thighs. Occasionally, he dips his fingers down and holds a piece of bacon or eggs or toast for me to nibble off him as he pets my head like I'm his loyal dog.

"Don't bite, now. Take it easy," he says, handing me another piece of bacon. As I eat it, his hands stroke my scalp and I relax into the sensation. "Good girl."

Once we finish up, I clean his dishes for him and am allowed some water and alone time to clean myself before he puts me in the crate. He doesn't tell me where he goes for the day, but I figure it's to work at the front desk.

Today, when he shoves me inside, he gives me a peck on the nose before he goes. I curl up for my nap…

It's dark by the time I wake and my stomach aches. Both from hunger and my uterus and just not feeling right. He's usually home by now.

What seems like hours pass, and the pain doesn't end and only gets worse until I *know* I'm just going to have to go all over my crate. At least there's newspaper down. Once I ruin my clothes, I use them to clean myself as much as I can, drink some water, and try to settle back down. My period may have ended now, as there isn't as much blood, only spots. And now that my belly isn't hurting, I have to try to sleep with the smell. Where is he?

Fear overtakes me several hours later. He's never left me this long, and I wonder if he knows what I've been planning. What if he found the slippers and sweatshirt? Is he leaving me down here to die?

I scream for help several times, but there's no sound from above. Light peeks through the window until it becomes day. Now, I'm terrified.

Sitting up, I grab the bars and try to pry them apart. They won't budge. Using my teeth, I tug at my paws, but the bindings are too tight. My heart thumps in my chest so hard I think I may have a heart attack, and just as I contemplate how I could end my own life with what little supplies I have before things get too dire, I hear a thud on the top step.

"Andy! Andy! Help!"

"Oh, my pet! Phew-y! It sure does stink down here. Did you go poo in your crate, Cherry girl?"

He edges to my side and slides open the lock, but before I can burst out, he holds me by the collar. "No, bad girl. You shouldn't use your newspaper like that." Taking a clean piece, he rolls it up, then swats my nose, the sensation more shocking than painful. Swiveling me toward the mess in the corner, he shoves my nose straight in it as I try to twist away. "Bad girl. Bad." Tugging on my collar, he pulls me out and I try to explain.

"You left me there all night!" All I can smell is my own mess, now caked on my face.

"Aww, did you miss your master?" Practically dragging me up the stairs, I beg for the shower to wash my face.

"Please, Andy. Let me clean up."

"Oh, we're bathing you for sure. But you need punishment." Once we get to the bathroom, he tosses me inside, but lays out another pair of panties and a T-shirt for me. "Don't put those on. You stay naked, except for your collar, when you come out here."

Taking my time, I pamper myself in the hot water. Scrubbing my face clean and between my legs, everything feels better with the comforts I took for granted when I lived at home.

Why hasn't Zack found me yet? Did he even try to look?

Worse… what is this punishment Andy is going to give me? Not wearing clothes anymore?

I towel off and use my fingers to comb through my hair. After brushing my teeth, he bangs on the door. "You're done. Get out here."

When I step into his room, he replaces my old collar with something different. "What is that?"

"New collar. Now… let's go." A wide palm shoves me between my shoulder blades until I hit the floor on all fours. He clips a leash to the back of my neck. I guess I can't walk any longer. Back to the old school dog days, I guess.

"What about my paws and foot pads?" I ask. Do I miss them? Not at all, but it makes me worry what his plans are. Did he just forget?

"You won't need those."

He leads me to the basement stairs and smacks my ass with an open palm after opening the door. "Move. Crawl down there."

Murmured voices filter up from the cinder block room that echo through the stairwell as I place a palm on the first step. When I turn my head to look back at Andy, he gives a small smile and nods. "Go on, pet. You've got visitors."

When I reach the bottom, I pause. The room is filled with naked men of all shapes, shades, heights, ages… But each wears a black ski mask and is choking their dicks. They all turn to me like I'm a feast about to be served to a host of hungry lions. One man whistles loudly, and the others cheer or laugh. Some yell obscenities I can barely make out.

Andy says, "Here's our pet! She's ready to be bred. Ain't that right, Cherry girl?"

My stomach sinks as I scan the eyes of the predators surrounding me. There's too many to count. Maybe twenty? Thirty?

A yank on my leash sends me forward, and I almost fall on my face, but keep crawling as the men part to let me glide by. Several reach down to pet my head, my back, my butt. One tries to stick his finger inside my asshole. I yelp and scurry forward.

In the center of the room, where I laid for Andy to remove my birth control, is the table with straps. Several men lift me as I kick against them, but it's no use.

"Hold her."

"Grab her."

"Someone take that arm. Tie her down."

"She's kicking!"

A cacophony of confusion rings in my ears as I'm forced to my back on the table, held down by a waist strap, arm straps and my legs in stirrups.

Andy bends to place his face next to mine, the crowd of riotous shouts dying down as he holds my gaze. "Precious pet. You'll suck dick in your mouth and take all our guests' cum in your cunt tonight and be the good breeding bitch you are, right? Or else..." He stands and a boisterous, almost unearthly laugh leaves his belly. "Chop, chop," he says, pointing to my arm.

"Andy... please. I love you. I-I..." I try to come up with some excuse, but he just brushes my hair back out of my face.

"Who's up first?" he asks, and a large man's gut presses between my wide-open thighs.

The stranger rubs his thin dick against my pussy folds,

then dribbles a strand of spit from his lips onto me, spreading it around with the crown. "I'm first for this dirty slut."

One hard shaft presses into my left palm, and as I turn to look, it thrusts between my lips. A little pat on my cheek warns me, along with a deep voice, "Open up."

Just as I do, the large man between my legs thrusts inside, and I gasp at his roughness. Another cock rubs into my right palm, then a hand pulls my face toward it.

With erratic grunts and shoves of his hips, the man inside me sputters a cough, and I squeeze my eyes shut instead of watching as he finishes, a string of cum trailing out as he pulls back. When he flops his soft cock on my mound, I get a peek of his satisfied eyes.

Another large and sweaty man slides in right after him, and the two near my face shuffle to get in line for my pussy. A few more replace them.

I grunt as the next man thrusts inside. He's much larger, and his fingers dig into my hips, but anytime I open my mouth to make a noise, one of the men near my head shoves inside.

My brain was counting how many there have been, but all I can see are the bodies immediately surrounding me. They all say gross things to me.

"Hungry little bitch, ain't ya?"

"Give it to this nasty slut."

One strokes my hair and bends down to whisper in my ear, "You're not even gonna know who the daddy is."

Sometimes, one of the animals gets too excited and breaks through the shoulders of the onlookers, then sprays my belly or face with warm reams of their pleasure. Closing my eyes so I don't get it in them, I try to use my tongue to wipe off as much as I can, but by the tenth or eleventh man, I can't do anything about it.

"Ugh, she's covered in cum. Dirty bitch."

Hands grope at my breasts constantly, stroking the nipples, pinching, tweaking. I wish they would stop, but it makes my clit throb at the same time. Occasionally, I'll feel the heat rising between my legs, but embarrassment has kept me from having an orgasm.

Until a man covered in silver hair presses his prominent gut into my legs. All I want to do is close my sore hip joints, but something about the way he works himself inside my slickness makes it tingle. His hands are gentler than the others and his eyes are crystal blue behind the mask. They seem kind.

"Such a beautiful girl. So young, too. Mm, been a while since I had such a young, tight pussy."

Breaking away from one of the dicks in my mouth, I catch my breath a moment, but am surprised at how turned on I am by the way he works me. "Call me grandpa, little girl."

Shockingly, the orgasm rips through me until I arch my back against the restraint holding my waist and yell, "Grandpa!"

"Good girl…"

As I come down from my high, I meet his kind eyes, and he pats my belly. "Good girl for letting us all use your holes," he says again, then hurries his speed and comes inside me. This one doesn't immediately pull out, though, and takes his time wandering away.

After that orgasm, the rest seem to come easier. In fact, something odd happens. The rough touches begin to feel good. My cheeks flush with desire, and my body feels sexy at their lewd comments. Instead of fighting my restraints, I start humping the cocks inside me, in every hole. Sometimes I suck their balls or jerk them off onto my breasts. One man even dips his lips to my nipple, licks off a trail of the white cream, and pinches my breast between his teeth as I climax on another man working through me.

Eventually, the line seems fewer, the voices quieter. Until there's only one man left and Andy, standing against the back wall, smoking a cigarette. Once each man finishes, they leave through the door to outside. The cold air has filtered in and leaves me shivering, lonely on the table.

I'm exhausted. I have no idea how many loads have filled me, but I'm covered in stranger's cum and sweat.

When the last man leaves, I think Andy will take his turn. Instead, he releases my binds. All of them, except my collar. Rolling to my side, I finally close my legs, everything spilling out of me and rolling in between my ass cheeks, dripping onto the table.

Andy scoops me into his arms, and I almost fall asleep at the sway of his footsteps as he carries me upstairs. "Forty-two," he whispers, and I peek an eye open to catch his soft expression. "You let forty-two men give you a cream pie. What a good breeding bitch you are. I'm so proud of you."

His lips press to the top of my head as he sets me inside his bathtub, which has been filled with warm water. Just as he did last week, he takes his time to wash every inch of me clean. As his fingers scrub my scalp, I finally give in to the sensation and fully relax.

As I fall asleep, I think… tomorrow is when I escape.

CHAPTER 6

My entire body jerks awake in surprise. I'm in a bed. *His* bed, not the dog bed or crate. Andy's chest presses against my bare back as he cuddles with me like I'm his girlfriend. His taut arm is thrown over my waist and a sculpted thigh lays protectively over mine.

It's difficult, but I take a languid inhale, pretending I'm still asleep. A reminder of yesterday's horrific events hits my hips and pussy as they throb with soreness.

I just got off my period. I'm fine, I'm fine. No babies. No babies.

I have to get out of here.

Edging as slowly as I can away from my captor, I scoot off the mattress. Once my feet hit the floor, my eyes dart to his face, but he doesn't move. I hurry to the closet, toss my sweatshirt and slippers on, then slide to the bedroom door. With one last glance back at him, I blow him a fake kiss, then sneak into the hall and carefully close the door behind me.

Scurrying toward the kitchen, I reach my hand toward the key rack and pause. My heart stops. There are no keys. Where did they go? He always keeps his car and house rings here!

Doom strikes my soul. He must have them in his pocket. I can't go back in there! Hurriedly, I unlock the back door and fling it open, sprinting into the early morning sunrise. The grass is slick with dew, and I almost slip, but aim for the woods leading down the hill to the motel. As I reach the tree line, a commotion behind me makes me turn my head.

Andy rampages out onto his back porch, his eyes narrowing when he spots me. Kicking the slippers off, I sprint between the trees. If I can just make it to the motel, maybe there's a chance I find someone on the road or at least call the police. My van should still be there.

Heavy footfalls behind me land about twenty yards away. Zig-zagging, I try to hide as much as I can from him. Instead of yelling, he silently follows at a brisk pace. Like he knows exactly where I'm going, and my efforts are useless. I don't care. I have to try.

Once I reach the edge where I think I can slide down, I pause. The hillside ends in a steep cliff of mud and rock. If I try to turn around, Andy will be there. Just as I turn to make a dive off the edge, my heart races. The parking lot of the motel holds *two* vehicles. My van and...

Zack's Mercedes. That's his custom Mercedes! He came for me!

His tall figure emerges from the driver's side as he steps out of the car.

Tears flood my eyes as I see him. I raise my arms to wave and yell, but just as I do, pain surges through my entire body, and I hit the ground. Curling on my side, I convulse violently in a seizure. Drool floods my mouth and out the sides of my lips. Once the pain stops, I'm left in a pool of exhausted muscles. My voice chokes out as I try to make a sound.

Andy's figure stomps near, then he pushes my shoulder, so I lay on my back. His lanky body looms over me. He's never really looked angry before. Not until this moment.

"Like your new collar, pet?" Seething, he clenches his jaw until his face turns red.

As I try to speak, my voice is cut off once again by the shock surrounding my neck. Writhing in the mud, I can only let my muscles twitch. Once they finally relax, my body fades into the slick ground beneath me as I pant for air. Andy kneels, trapping me with his thighs, then tugs up my sweatshirt. Loosening his jeans, he pulls out his cock.

"Shh. Good puppy. Don't speak. Not unless you want shocked again." Gripping my hips, he lines up and rubs himself between my pussy lips, then dips his cock onto the dew grass beneath us. Terrified of the returning confusion and humming pain the collar may cause, I don't dare move.

With a formidable thrust, he fills me whole, and we both grunt at the connection. After only a few shoves, he pulls out, grabs my waist with a taut forearm, and flips me over until my face hits the dirt. Yanking hard on my thighs, he pulls me up to meet his hard thickness again.

"Oof!" I say, then clamp my mouth closed. It's not just wanting to keep quiet to avoid the shock; I also swallow mud each time my lips part.

One hand pressed to the back of my head, he punches into my hips with his repeatedly. Surely, I'll bruise. I hate that he feels so good.

Gripping my hair, he lifts me up so I'm staring down the mountain at my husband wandering around the motel.

"You see that man? He thinks he's your owner, but you know better, don't you? Huh?" With a sharp snap, he spanks my ass until I nod, tears falling from my face.

"Tell him goodbye. You have a new master now. One that knows how to keep you." My breath catches as he rails into me. Swiveling back into him, the heat climbs through my core and settles in between my thighs.

"Tell him, Cherry girl." Tugging me back into his chest, he whispers in my ear, "Tell him goodbye and that you love me."

A sob escapes. Is it goodbye? Will I never see him again? Is my fate now with the man inside me giving me insane pleasure?

"Go-goodbye, Zack. I have a new master now. I love him." Hot water drips from my eyes onto my cheeks.

Another spank makes me gasp until I sniff my running nose. "Good girl. And tell him how much better I fuck you. Say how much bigger my dick is compared to his."

"So-so much bigger, Andy. You-you fuck me better."

A flashback of Zack and I making love gently on our sofa after a Saturday night movie invades my mind. He used to care about giving me orgasms. Then he stopped. After we'd finish, I'd have to get myself off with my toys. Sometimes he'd say he would help, but then he'd fall asleep.

Oddly, this absolute psychopath makes me come hard. Andy lowers my head into the grass once again and fucks me like an animal. The sensation causing tingles to rip up and down my spine with pleasure.

"That's my bitch. My nasty slut taking so many cum shots in her pussy, she probably has seven or eight pups in there now. Ugh... You love being a fucking whore, don't you?" When he swats my ass cheek, I moan yes, and let my climax invade every piece of me. Andy forces my head up as Zack gets back in his car. "Scream that you love me. Scream it. You're not his anymore."

My inner muscles clench onto the firm rod working me from behind as I yell that I love Andy, but as my voice leaves my chest, another seizure hits. All my body stiffens around him as he continues to pump inside me. I have no control, but the tightening locks my brain into such ecstasy, I feel blissfully high.

"Yes, pet. Fuck, you're so tight like this. Ouch! Got me a

little, too, you dirty minx." Then he laughs riotously as he comes inside me.

When the shock ends, I splash like liquid onto the grass and he slips out of me, dragging some of his juices with him.

Andy drags me by the collar with one finger hooked round my neck. I can't even move, so it's more like I'm skating through the mud. My knees get caught on a twig, so he grabs my hair and tugs until I moan with the agony of it ripping from my skull. I scramble onto my knees, attempting to catch up with him. He tosses me down the side stone steps and into the basement. My stomach twists into a knot knowing... This is it for me.

He's going to take my arm off for trying to escape.

But all he does is open my crate and throw me inside.

As he slams the metal door shut with a clang, his fierce gray eyes meet me. "Listen here. You deserve punishment."

"Please, Andy. Please don't cut off my arm! I'll do anything. I'm so sorry."

With vitriol spitting from his mouth, he says, "I told you. I don't want no three-legged dog. Got something better in mind that always gets the bitches to act right. Enjoy your solitude."

Then he spins on his heel and goes up the stairs, shutting off the light to leave me in semi-darkness. At least there's the window. My new home is safer than what he may do to me. Does this mean he's leaving me alone?

Will I starve down here?

IT SEEMS AS IF IT'S ABOUT A DAY AND A HALF BEFORE HE returns. It's dark when he does. Thirst is overwhelming my senses, but my hunger has lessened to annoyance. For the last six or so hours of calculating the sun's movement, I've been sobbing dry tears, thinking he left me to die. And now that his footsteps pound on the wooden stairs, relief floods me for my captor.

I'm desperate for him.

But my chest tightens when I hear another sound...

Delicate footsteps patter behind him, and as he rounds the corner, a broad smile forms on his lips. Just as I think it's for me, he turns his head to greet his guest.

A small blonde woman that I hope is eighteen follows him down the steps in a tiny leather skirt and combat boots, fishnet stockings, and ribbons trailing in her pigtails. Never once looking at me, she focuses on the man in front of her. He grabs her around the waist, then leans in to kiss her lips passionately. The two cling to each other like they are long lost lovers.

The sight of them makes my stomach cramp, not just from wanting to eat. Shifting up to a sitting position, I monitor their movements carefully as he dances her lithe body to the middle of the room where the table I was strapped to still stands.

Too afraid to speak, I hold my tongue. Does she know? Is she aware what hell dimension she just stepped into?

As if she doesn't have a care in the world, she lets him take off her cropped T-shirt and tosses her hair back with a little giggle. *A giggle,* as if she's here willingly. Am I so far gone I'm hallucinating?

He helps her undress slowly, sensually, caressing her skin with his fingers delicately while kissing her every place he can reach. As he drips off pieces of his own clothing, he makes his way to the center of the floor. "Just a sec, precious. Let me get my pet."

The girl takes a peek at me, with superiority written all over her face. She licks her bottom lip and almost laughs as

Andy drags me from the crate. Moving toward her, he grabs my hair and holds my cheek against his thigh.

"Suck me, pretty girl. On your knees."

The woman does as he says while keeping her seductive eyes trained on his face, then swallows his cock in her little mouth. As she licks the tip, fear strikes me that Andy's replaced me. Does this mean I'm done for? Will he chop me up and put me in the drain?

I wonder how badly it will hurt.

"You're so big," the girl laughs, then gags on him as he thrusts in between her pert lips. While I lounge on him, he strokes my hair as if I'm a dog. All I can do is watch her work his length, but with every stroke, my anxiety turns to some odd jealousy. The way he's almost gentle with her and stroking her cheek with his thumb. How she's clearly enjoying it. Do I have to kill her to stay alive? Could I even *do* that?

"Here, pet. Eat my ass while this good girl sucks my dick."

My belly flops. Did he say… eat his ass? I almost speak because I don't know what that means. I haven't ever done something like that. Nausea floods the back of my throat, wondering how dirty he is. But I want to prove to him my worth. Make sure he keeps me around and doesn't bring his machete anywhere near me.

So, while his hips jut forward, I get behind him and lick carefully one stroke between his cheeks. My tongue is almost dry, which disguises any flavor I may sense. Andy lifts his thigh onto the table in front of him, grasps the girl's head, then reaches around to do the same to mine, pressing my face into his crack.

"Stick your tongue in there, pet. Fuck it with your mouth. Suck my asshole."

Hurriedly, I obey. Sticking my tongue out, it's dampened with his sweat. I ignore the taste and thrust inside his tight ring. Fortunately, he's not as disgusting as I was expecting, and the sound of his deep moans makes me settle into the task. In fact, I get so lost in it, I use my paws to spread his cheeks wider, sticking my nose deeper inside.

"F-fuck, pet, yes. Get up here, baby. Let me fuck this tiny cunt." The girl rises and slides on all fours on the table.

Andy pulls me away from his ass and straddles my head, so I'm stuck looking at the base of his cock, about to enter this girl. "Suck my balls while I fuck her pretty pussy."

Watching him slide into the other woman makes me unexpectedly rage inside. That's what *I'm* for. If he's replacing me, that means I'm finished.

Not only that, but I thought Andy loved *me*. I'm his pet. I'm his! He said so!

"Fuck, she's so tight. Lick my taint there, slut. When I come inside her, I want you to eat it. Eat my cream pie, pet. Suck it out of her tiny twat."

Anger surges through me, but I do as he says, holding his balls in my mouth, even humming as he groans with his release. As if this girl matters to him, he scoops her up and kisses her longingly on the mouth, lapping sounds echoing through the room for minutes, while he stays tucked deep inside her. She whimpers against his lips. My view of them is half blocked by her pussy and his thighs, but when he finally releases her, a clump of thick cum drizzles from her hole toward my waiting mouth.

"Eat it, pet. Eat my cum."

Twisting, I shove my face onto her shaved cunt and suck up every drop. I've never eaten pussy, but she tastes like Andy, which makes me almost ravenous. I'm terribly thirsty, and her wetness coats my face as I dive in. Slurping every bit of their sex up, I lick my lips clean. She can't have any of it.

And as if Andy knows exactly what I was thinking, he

says, "That's right, pet. It's yours. Eat your master's cum. It belongs to you, right?"

Sliding back to sit on my butt, I gaze up at him and nod proudly.

"Stick out your tongue for me."

I do, showing him my empty mouth. He grips my chin and smiles broadly. "Such a good girl."

With a smack on the girl's ass, she climbs off the table and dresses. He carts me back into my crate and pulls on his own clothes. The two of them head up the stairs, and Andy tosses his arm over her shoulders, giving her a light peck on the temple. But as he does…

He looks at me.

I think I'm in love with Andy.

CHAPTER 7

ANDY

I didn't think I could love her more, but when she willingly ate my cum out of my sister's cunt, it just solidified how superb she is for me.

My perfect pet.

I've brought out the best in her. The extra thickness she carried on her hips when she arrived has slimmed to a toned, sleek look of the finest breeding stock.

It's taken years to learn the right balance. Some struggled to birth when they were too fat.

But not my Cherry.

She's Westminster cup worthy in her beauty.

Taking the mongrel that arrived, through my love and devotion, she's transformed into a pedigreed specimen.

If only I could keep her from fucking running, I'd take her to my puppy mill.

There's still a nip behind her words, but she's learning.

"Good morning, pet. You've been obeying so well since my sister visited last month. Are you ready for a walk?" Opening her cage, she crawls weakly out on the stained concrete.

How long did I leave her in this time?

I get so distracted with the other breeders.

"Yes, master." Her voice cracks dryly, but she sits back on her knees obediently for my leash.

Benevolence is one of my strongest virtues. Perhaps I'll reward her.

"Have your breakfast, and then I have a surprise for you." Unzipping my jeans, I let my semi-hard cock free for her to guzzle.

The leather of her paws is worn smooth and they slide up my denimed thighs easily.

When she takes me into her hot mouth, I get the shiver I crave run through my belly.

Her parched lips stick to my stiffening skin, but she diligently tries to take me deeper.

It makes me hard, seeing her struggle.

"Lean your muzzle back." My thumb finds the hollow beneath her chin, pushing her face up to watch me. "Open."

Look at her, doing what she's told without hesitation.

I think she's ready.

Swirling my tongue, I pull a ball of saliva free from my cheeks and let it drop in a long string to her waiting hole.

She doesn't blink as it pools against the back of her throat.

"Continue."

Those eyes do me in every time when she stares up at me.

Longingly.

My Cherry needed this discipline. She was too wild for too long.

Breaking her into this sweet, domestic house bitch has been the best thing that has ever happened to her.

I saved her.

She sucks with fervor as the head of my cock mushrooms. Fuck, she knows exactly what to do. Licking that tender spot just below the tip, she vacuums my length into the vise of her neck.

I can feel her trying to gag around me, but she stays lodged over my shaft, swallowing every drop that erupts from my burning balls.

When the last shiver leaves my body, she sits back, but makes no move to wipe the tears, snot, or dribbles of cum from her mottled face.

"That's it. You've earned a new home, girl." Patting the top of her head, gesture for her to follow.

She pauses almost imperceptibly before pushing herself to her feet and padding behind me.

Hmm. A well-trained pet never hesitates.

At the top of the stairs, I veer toward the living room. "Get some food and go potty. We're going for a ride."

"Where, um—" Her words jumble. "Did I do something wrong, master?" She doesn't delay in her movements, only tossing her question over her shoulder as she fills her water bowl in the sink.

She knows better than to not do what I ask.

"No, pet. You're graduating." Folding myself into the recliner, I let one leg dangle over the arm while I text my father.

The stiff plastic in my pocket reminds me.

"Oh, Cherry. I nearly forgot." Pushing open the bathroom door, I catch her just as she's squatting onto the toilet.

Pulling the thin stick free, I hand it to her with a small flourish. "Use this."

Her delicate fingers brush mine before her dark brows furrow. "Is it, um, is this what I think it is, master?"

She tugs the cap from the end, revealing the test strip hidden within.

"Time to see if you have a litter coming. Only breeders

get to leave." Leaning against the frame, I settle in to watch her.

Her eyes widen, looking up, then shift to the floor.

"I'm not leaving until I know." The tingle in my crotch almost begs her not to be settled. I want to make her womb suckle my cock again and again.

Nodding, she pulls her swollen bottom lip between her teeth as she tucks her wrist between her thighs.

The bated silence is broken by her stream of acrid urine splashing into the water beneath her.

She sets the soiled test on the edge of the counter, noticeably avoiding looking at it.

My heart beats faster when I see the faded line appear.

"You're such a good girl. Who do you think the sire of your pups will be?" Cupping her face, I watch the tremble of her nostril.

She's fighting so hard to be what I want.

It's hard to overcome poor habits. We've come so far in making her behave, and this is worth a small victory lap.

"I hope it's you, master." A muscle next to her left eye twitches in a tiny pulse.

"Really? And why is that?" Tracing my finger down her cheek, I let my palm rest against the racing beat of her heart in her throat.

"Because I love you, Andy." Cherry drops her gaze demurely, but I can feel the rapid leap of her breathing.

I wonder.

"Finish grooming yourself. We'll leave soon." Stepping away is best. There will be time to fuck her back into submission later.

Her crisp, clean scent precedes her as I finish making her treat.

"That smells delicious, master." Folding her hands behind

her back, she bends to her water bowl and laps from the stainless reservoir.

"I told you, giving me a litter earns you special privileges." Peeling back the foil of the dish reveals the steaming salmon I've heated for her. "This is for doing what you're told. See how well I take care of you?"

Her smile almost appears genuine. "Yes, you do, master." Dropping to her heels, she begs me with her eyes.

My cock hardens, and I'm tempted to give her that instead. "You're so beautiful, pet. It makes me want to beat those babies out of you so I can fuck you pregnant all over again."

I pick up a morsel of the pink flesh. I hold it to her puffy mouth where she slowly suctions the flaky bite.

Exquisite.

When the filet is nothing but a few bones and skin, I gather her leash from the wall. "It's time."

I'm not going to make the same mistake and let her run loose outside, no matter how tempting it is to shock her until she voids herself again.

She's shaking, but she minds.

Loading her into the crate in the back of my van, I double check to make sure that no one can see her through the windows.

I've learned from my previous errors.

The drive is a path I make daily. She travels well, quietly. Her training is remarkable.

She's a prime addition.

"Come, pet." I let her walk beside me, rather than behind, so I can showcase her when we enter.

I want the rest to see her.

"It's about time." Rachel crosses her arms and scowls at me when we push through the double doors.

"Don't pout, sis. Or I'll bend you over in front of the

buyers and show them what a *real* slut looks like." The leash around my wrist tightens.

My pet has balked away from my gorgeous sister.

Perhaps threatened?

Rachel's face slackens into a wide smile. Tossing her blond hair over her shoulder, her arms open and wrap around my neck. "My, my, brother. It seems your little toy is put off by me." Her hot breath works over my jaw as her lips tighten onto the lobe of my ear. "Is she jealous? So adorable. The customers like shy."

Fuck, she makes me hard. "She's bred. I'm not done with her, yet." Dragging her knee up my thigh, I open her like the forbidden flower she is to dip my fingers into her bare pussy. "Like I'm going to do to you if you keep rubbing my cock that way."

The heat of her touch has me throbbing.

"Come find me after your showing. I'll be waiting for you." She squeezes my balls firmly and then saunters away, her luscious hips swaying with each enticing step.

A growl escapes me as I tug Cherry to follow.

She keeps tension on the tether, slowing at every pen we pass.

I wave my hand in an idle gesture. "Don't mind them, pet. You'll have your own. No more sharing until it's breeding season again."

Through the warehouse, she still tries to peer into the stalls that house my other specimens.

The high dollar ones are kept near the end in opulent rooms that fulfill all of their needs.

My finest stock.

"We'll see how the bidding goes. You may earn one of these. Would you like that?" Jerking her collar seems to reset her attention back to me.

"Y-yes, master." Tears well in her eyes before they stain

her cheeks. "All of them." She gestures with one of her leather paws. "They're all like me?"

Fear quakes in the clear droplet that falls from her lip.

"None of them can compare to you. Your confirmation is ideal. I can promise that you'll be the most valuable of them all." I brush the dampness from her chin and pull her close.

My fingers are still slick from my sister when I push them into Cherry's tight cunt. "This hole deserves to have an army of followers. Just imagine who will be lucky enough to own one of your litter."

A gasp flutters against my skin as she looks around wildly. The blush working up her chest, and the tiny pants she struggles to fight, prove how much she longs for my touch.

"Don't worry, pet. They've all seen how well you take forty-two cocks. If we're fortunate, it's a girl bedded in you. Let's go show you off, and then I'll make you come." Circling her clit with my thumb, I can feel her hips spasm in rhythm to my strokes. "Would you like that?"

She whimpers into my shirt. "Yes, master."

"Good girl." I let my hand drop and turn, pulling her leash.

Her legs wobble as she follows, the flush of arousal painting her skin.

After I drag the heavy steel door open, I guide her in to stand on the illuminated dias in the center of the black room.

"Stand here until I tell you." I unclip the lead, but ready the remote to her collar in my pocket.

Just in case.

She jumps when the voice breaks through the speakers, making her bare breasts bounce with her movements.

"Up next, lot 576. Confirmed positive. Sire unknown." The rapid-fire words turn into a soothing cadence I've grown used to.

I was right. She's a royal crown. I've never heard the bidding get that high before.

When the final gavel hits, she collapses in the center of the stage, her paws covering her face.

"You did amazing." I stroke the top of her head before snapping the leash back in place.

"But, am I still yours?" She pushes herself up to stand, but her shoulders slump as she follows me.

"You'll always be mine. It's your pups I've just auctioned. You did such a wonderful job out there. I'm very proud." Walking ahead of her, I'm slowed by her dragging steps.

"My-my baby?" Blood crests from her lower lip as she bites it. "What are they… What will they do?"

Shrugging, I jerk the line to hurry her. "Everyone wants a pet like you, Cherry."

We come to the end of the quiet hall, and I pull her into the small room near the main exit.

"Sit." I point to the chair in the center under a large exam light.

She slides obediently into the stiff seat. Strapping her arms down with the thick velcro attached only takes seconds.

I've done this a few times.

"There's only one more thing. You're going to be staying in this kennel, and I can't have you barking. Open your mouth."

I hate that she hesitates.

My fingers dig into her jaw, forcing her to widen the gap between her teeth.

"Do you love me?" Picking up the tool I need, I wait for her response.

"Yeth." Her tongue sticks out between her lips, making her lisp.

The clamp grabs hold of the tip so I can pry it further out of her mouth.

"Remember that it's the last words you'll say. My precious." Wedging her head against the backrest, the hotknife is already searing before I slice through the meaty center.

Her scream gurgles with the blood that runs into the back of her throat.

The dismembered muscle still twitches in the pliers when I toss it onto the tray.

Through muffled cries, she writhes against the restraints as red-stained saliva trails down her chin.

"Only one more thing, then I can take you to your new pen." Where is it?

I just need to find my RFID gun. She would be lost if she became a stray.

Squatting, I pull the cabinet open. It's usually kept here.

Maybe it's behind this—

A hard slam against my temple stuns me.

Pain explodes into bright lights in my vision.

Another strike knocks me backward, and I blink at the blinding light.

Cherry silhouettes against the glare, the heavy tray in her hands.

I try to raise my hand weakly to block the next blow, but I'm not fast enough.

Darkness swallows me.

CHAPTER 8

The pain is almost blinding, but my mind surges with adrenaline to run. Just run. Keep my legs moving, pumping. Far away. As far from here as I can get.

Blood gushes from my mouth with every stumbled step, so I leave my lips parted until it all spills down my chin. My tongue is gone! I have no tongue! How can I talk or eat or anything?

Autumn air cuts like knives across my skin as I burst from the warehouse door, searching for Andy's van among the sea of pickup trucks lining the gravel lot. It's easy to spot the large white vehicle. I dart and dive between shorter cars, ducking when I see men loitering near the side of the metal shed.

Reaching the driver's door, I tug, and relief floods my chest as it opens easily. When I jump inside, tears flood my eyes as my paw grasps at the ignition. The keys are still here.

With a violent scream of terror and victory, I start the engine. It's difficult to hold the steering wheel with the leather mitts in the way, but at this point, I'd rather crash than go back to that madhouse.

I can't think about all the ways my mind has been warped over the last month, but one of the worst is the hurt and betrayal by the man I thought loved me. Rachel is *his sister,* and they are clearly together. Andy has other women just like me. Stocked away like breeding stock.

I was never just his. I wasn't his special pup like I thought. And that I even care makes me vomit some blood onto the carpeted interior next to my seat.

A sob escapes as I pull out of the lot in a hurry, some of the men chasing after the tailgate as the tires kick up stones. The side view mirrors cloud with dust as the image of their angry faces disappears into the distance when I gun it onto the main road.

I have no idea where I'm heading, but I'm not stopping until I find some place *safe*. Though a nagging fear inside my chest says I'm not even sure that exists anymore. Maybe there's a police station. This town seems too tiny for a hospital.

It's so difficult to turn the wheel but I throw it left when I spot a gas station. An old one with rusted white pumps and a sad open sign on the door. Naked, cold, and bloody, I jump out while leaving the motor running and sprint inside, thrusting open the glass door.

A teenage boy with black hair's eyes widen as he spots me. "Oh my god… Stay back. Don't come any closer! I'll shoot!" He… he's afraid of *me?* Reaching beneath the counter, he pulls up a shotgun and tries to hold it, but it's clear he doesn't know how.

Making the motion of a phone, I scream, "Po-ee! Po-ee! Haaaaaaap!" But the screaming only seems to terrify the kid more. I must look like a zombie.

Instead of staying to get shot, I dart back to the van. What if no one helps me?

There's nothing I can find to cover myself in it, and so, I

dart off down the road further. There are a couple of fast-food places and finally I spy a fire station, small, but formidable.

And next to it is a police station...

Parking in front, I jump out and sprint inside, unable to contain my moaning cries now. Once my pads hit the hardwood of the little interior entry, I collapse and curl into a ball. I can't do this anymore. I'm done. Someone needs to take me.

"What in the world? Someone call the deputy on duty. Help me with her!" a motherly voice calls out and loud shuffling and yelling surround my ears. "Oh, dear. Hold tight. I'm going to get you a blanket. Have you been shot? What's the matter, dear...?" She calls over her shoulder, "I think she's been shot. There's blood."

Rubbing my upper arm, I stare at her brown loafers as she squats near me. In a moment, she tosses a thick blanket over me and has a water bottle in hand. "Can you sit? What happened?"

Raising myself to my hip, I take the water from her and use it to wipe off some of the blood. She hands me a towel, and I try to speak, "Ma, ma, ma..." It's all I can say.

"Oh, my word... Shelby! Someone cut her mouth! Shelby! Where's the deputy?" She pats my hand and tears fill her eyes. "He'll take you to the hospital, baby. You poor thing. We need to know who did this to you."

Another bleached blonde woman comes bounding back into the room, frantic and pacing. "He said he'd be right here. He's on his way. Let's get her into the office."

"Can you walk, dear?"

Nodding, I sniff, and the blonde hands me some tissues. Holding my bottle, towel, and tissues like treasures, they help me up and stand on either side of me as I walk to a back room.

The walls are constructed of old paneled wood, and it smells of cigarettes, but I collapse into a plastic chair in front of a cluttered desk. A phone from up front begins ringing.

"The deputy should be right here. I have to go answer that phone. Shelby, go to the fire station and see if any of them are near right now…" Her lips form a solid line as her brow furrows. "I'm so sorry. We only have volunteers here. We got a small town."

I suddenly regret every decision I've made in the last two years. Mainly Brandon and hurting Zack. He came for me. I wonder if he's still alive or if Andy did something to him, too.

All those women locked in cages… without tongues like me.

My mind feels like a jumbled mess, and I just want to sleep. Sleep for fifty years or maybe never wake up if it's still in this nightmare.

The glass door of the station opens, and the nice lady greets someone, who murmurs back to her. She tells them I'm in the office.

As the footsteps approach, I relax completely. My rescuer is here. The hospital… Maybe there's something that can be done.

I could start fresh and turn my life around now.

Shuffles stop dramatically as the person behind me stops in the doorway suddenly.

Turning my head, I see *him*. My master, my owner… all decked out in a policeman's uniform.

"Well, hello, pet," Andy says.

THE END

ACKNOWLEDGMENTS

Thank you to M.A. Cobb for your guidance in making this horror novella *horrific*. I couldn't have pushed over the edge I needed to without you. You truly brought Andy to life with chapter 7.

Thank you to my REAM Queens for subscribing and reading along every month. Your support is invaluable, as are your comments on the stories as I post them. I live for those instant reactions you give me!

Thank you to my beta team for doing amazing work, as always.

ABOUT THE AUTHOR

Kitty King is a bestselling romance writer and a psychiatrist. She is the author of the International bestseller *Red Night: Xavier's Delight*. Kitty enjoys reading erotic romance tales just as much as writing them. She isn't sure she has the stomach to write another horror novella. But had so much fun…it'll probably still happen.

https://kittykingauthor.com

Milton Keynes UK
Ingram Content Group UK Ltd.
UKHW040727090924
448088UK00001B/14

9 781964 647098